For Harry, Izzy, Isaac and Arthur

CHAPTER ONE
AMELIA'S HOUSE

There was something about his best friend's home that made Ethan nervous. Amelia's house was bigger than his, and even from the outside it looked very fancy. The front lawn and hedges were neatly trimmed, and the wide driveway led to a double garage. A gravel path wound to the bright white front door which had a shiny knocker in the middle. Ethan had to stand on his toes to reach it. The sharp crack-crack-crack rang in his ears as he banged.

Ethan and Amelia hadn't been friends for long and it was the first time he'd been over to her house.

"Hello!" Amelia's mum said when she opened the door.

"Hi, Mrs Hopton." Ethan glanced behind

her. The house was so clean and tidy that it made Ethan feel messy. He pushed his hand over his hair to try and neaten it up. It always stuck out all over the place.

Amelia's mum didn't work so she was always at home to look after Amelia and her brother and sister. Their home life was very different to Ethan's. At his house it was just him and his dad.

"Come in," Mrs Hopton said, standing aside and calling up the stairs for Amelia.

Ethan looked around as he stepped into the hallway. The polished wooden table against the wall had matching ornaments on it - two black horses which stood reared on their back legs. Between them was a framed photo of the whole family, all of them smiling into the camera.

"You can put your coat in here," Mrs Hopton said, pressing a panel under the staircase to reveal a hidden cupboard.

Ethan shrugged his coat off and put it away.

From the hall he could see into the kitchen, where a baby sat banging on a pan with a wooden spoon.

"Not so loud, Abigail," Mrs Hopton called to her, then shouted up to Amelia again. She shook her head and walked towards the kitchen, leaving Ethan wondering what to do.

"Hi!" Amelia said, leaning over the bannister at the top of the stairs. "Come up."

He'd just put a foot on the first stair when Amelia's mum came back with the baby on her hip. "Shoes go in here," she said, pressing a different panel to pop out a large drawer with rows of shoes.

"Sorry," he mumbled, easing his feet from his scruffy trainers and shoving them onto the rack.

"I'll bring snacks up in a little while," Amelia's mum said when he was halfway up the stairs. "And I'd like you to play outside later to get some fresh air."

"I can open the window for fresh air," Amelia said, her black hair swinging around her as she leaned further over the bannister.

"You need exercise too," Mrs Hopton said. "And don't lean so far over the stairs. One of these days you'll fall. Have you brushed your hair today?"

"Yes," Amelia said.

"Well, brush it again. And tie it up."

"No," Amelia said, sounding annoyed. "It's my hair, I'll wear it how I want. I don't tell you what to do with your hair."

Ethan continued up the stairs, wondering if Amelia would get into trouble for talking to her mum like that. But Mrs Hopton just tutted and walked away.

On the landing, Ethan glanced into a room to the left where an older boy sat in front of a computer with headphones on.

"That's Jacob," Amelia said. "He's allowed to

be on the computer as much as he wants and I don't think it's fair."

"How old is he?" Ethan asked. He'd seen Jacob around sometimes but didn't know anything about him.

"Thirteen. He's really annoying," Amelia said loudly.

Jacob rolled across the room on the desk chair. "I heard that," he said, then smiled at Ethan before closing the door on them.

"I've no idea what we're going to do here all day," Amelia said, walking to the room at the end of the hall. "It's much more fun at your house." She glanced back at Jacob's bedroom and lowered her voice. "I suppose I can show you where I hide my glass dragon at least."

CHAPTER TWO
AMELIA'S BEDROOM

Just like the rest of the house, Amelia's room was clean and tidy. Everything seemed to have a place. Not like at Ethan's house where things were left all over.

He looked in wonder at the wall which was completely covered in bookshelves. To him it seemed as though she had a whole library in her bedroom.

Amelia reached up to pull two books from a shelf. After feeling around in the space, she pulled out a small drawstring pouch. She put the books back, then tipped up the little bag until the glass dragon fell onto her palm.

Silently, Ethan and Amelia gazed at the orange dragon. It seemed to shimmer with magic. Ethan thought of his green dragon at home and wished he'd brought it with him.

"I'd really like to squeeze it now and disappear to Steorra," Amelia sighed.

Ethan longed to go on an adventure to Steorra too. The magical land of stars was so exciting. No one else knew about it and Ethan was glad he had Amelia to share the secret with.

"I didn't bring my dragon," Ethan said. "So we can't go. And I don't want to get into trouble. Or get found out and never be able to go again."

"I was only kidding," Amelia said. "We definitely can't go today. My mum watches me all the time. You're so lucky to have your house to yourself all day."

Ethan didn't think he was lucky at all. Before his dad had given him the glass dragons he'd always been lonely at home on his own in the holidays.

"It's boring sometimes," he said.

Moving to the window, he looked down at the kids who'd come out to play from the houses nearby. Even though he'd made friends with Amelia, he still got a funny feeling in his stomach when he watched the other kids play on their bikes and scooters. Ethan didn't have a bike so he'd always felt he couldn't join them. He'd tried a few times but they'd teased him so much that he'd given up.

"I don't know how it's boring to be able to do whatever you want, whenever you want," Amelia said. "My mum's always nagging me about something. It's like her hobby. Nagging!"

Ethan stared out of the window to avoid looking at Amelia. It was strange to think the things that annoyed Amelia were things that Ethan would like to have. Having a mum and a busy house sounded lovely to him.

"I hid this here too," Amelia said.

Ethan turned to see her pull a piece of paper from between two books. He smiled as he looked at the sparkling party invitation in the shape of a snowflake. Their friend Pascal had given it to them last time they were in Steorra. Ethan's sadness faded away as he thought about the penguin's birthday party at the end of the week.

"I can't wait," he said excitedly.

"I'm making him a hat and scarf." Amelia picked up the knitting from her desk. The scarf wasn't finished and the needles were still attached.

Ethan looked at the star pattern on the hat. "I didn't think about taking him a gift. I don't have anything."

"We'll say it's from both of us," Amelia said, then opened a wardrobe which was filled with board games.

They were sitting on the bed, in the middle of a game of Snap when Amelia's mum came in with a tray. Ethan's eyes lit up at the array of fruit, all neatly cut up. And orange juice and biscuits too.

"Have something to eat," Mrs Hopton said as she slid the tray onto the desk. "Then you can go out and play." She looked at Amelia. "We bought that brand-new bike for your birthday and you've barely ridden it. Why don't the two of you go for a bike ride?"

"I haven't got a bike," Ethan said quietly.

Mrs Hopton waved a hand in front of her face. "Borrow one of Jacob's old ones. There are so many bikes in that garage. Just make sure you find helmets too."

"Can't we stay inside?" Amelia asked.

"No. It's a beautiful day. You should go out and play with the other kids."

"Fine," Amelia said, then got up and took a piece of apple. She crunched on it noisily. When her mum left she turned to Ethan. "We'll have to go out, I suppose. Do you know *how* to ride a bike?"

"Yes." He took the plate of fruit that she held out to him and tucked in. "I had a bike when I was younger but I got too big for it and dad couldn't afford a new one."

"We've got loads of bikes but I hate playing outside. The kids are mean."

Ethan knew the other kids picked on Amelia and called her a vampire because of her jet-black hair which made her skin look pale. They teased him too because his last name was Broom and his dad worked as a street cleaner. They often joked that he should be cleaning too.

Ethan hated being teased. He'd never thought it bothered Amelia very much but maybe it did really. She was frowning as she ate.

Ethan went to the window to look out again.

Hopefully the kids wouldn't tease them today.

CHAPTER THREE
PLAYING OUTSIDE

E than couldn't believe it when he followed Amelia into the garage. In a bike rack, four bikes were neatly parked - one of them with a baby seat on the back. Behind them, on the far wall, was a stack of slightly dusty-looking bikes which obviously hadn't been ridden for a while.

"That's so cool," Ethan said as he stood looking at a black BMX bike.

"Take it," Amelia said. "See if it's the right size. We have to wear helmets or Mum will kill me." She plucked one from the shelf and handed it to Ethan.

He put it on and clicked the strap into place under his chin. Then he wheeled the bike out and tried it for size. It was perfect.

"I'm quite glad we didn't get to go to Steorra today," he called over his shoulder to Amelia.

"Why?" she asked, giving him a look that seemed to say she thought he was crazy.

"I never get to go bike riding."

"It's boring."

"Only because you can go whenever you want."

"So can you now," Amelia said. "You can borrow it any time."

"Thanks." He was happy that Amelia never cared that he lived in a messy house and didn't have cool new toys.

Not long ago he'd thought they could never be friends because they were so different. But making friends with Amelia had been one of the best things to happen to him. Their trips to Steorra was the other good thing.

Ethan straddled the bike and wobbled as he set off. Even though he remembered how to ride he still felt a little shaky.

Their street was a dead end so they didn't get many cars driving on it. The other kids were riding around in the road. Two of the boys were in Ethan's class at school. One boy, Zac, stopped in front of Ethan.

"New bike?" he asked.

"I borrowed it," Ethan replied.

"It's pretty cool. Can you do any tricks or jumps?"

Ethan frowned. "No."

An older boy called Freddie rode quickly towards them, then skidded to a stop. "Are you friends with the vampire now?" he asked, looking over Ethan's shoulder at Amelia.

Ethan's heart sped up and he wanted to say something but he didn't know what.

"Go away," Amelia said, sounding bored rather than angry. "This is my driveway and you're not allowed on it."

"What are you going to do about it?" Freddie asked.

"Bite your neck and suck your blood," she hissed, baring her teeth.

"Weirdo," Freddie said, then rode away with Zac following after him.

"You didn't want to play with them, did you?" Amelia asked Ethan.

"No," he said with a shrug.

"Let's ride down to the woods and get away from them," Amelia said.

He followed after her, peddling hard to keep up. When the houses came to an end, a rough path led into the trees. They kept going until they reached a small stream with large rocks scattered around it.

"Sometimes I come here when my house is too noisy," Amelia said.

Ethan threw a stick into the water. "My house is never too noisy."

"It's so much better when we play at your house," Amelia said as she sat beside the water and threw pebbles into the stream. "I can't wait to get back to Steorra."

"We'll go again soon," Ethan said, sitting beside her. "How do you think penguins celebrate their birthdays?"

"I've no idea," she said. "I guess they eat fish. And maybe go swimming."

Ethan shook his head. "Not Pascal. He hates swimming, remember?"

"Oh, yeah. I wonder what Pascal *does* like to do."

"I guess we'll find out soon," Ethan said, grinning.

CHAPTER FOUR
BACK IN STEORRA

"You're early," Ethan said when he opened the door to Amelia on Thursday morning. His dad had only just left for work.

"I can't find Pascal's invitation," Amelia said, stepping inside. "And I couldn't remember what time the party is."

"You lost the invitation?" Ethan asked, feeling a little panicky.

Amelia shrugged her shoulders. "It'll be somewhere in my room."

"What if your mum found it?" he asked.

If her mum had read the invitation she'd start asking questions. Ethan was terrified of someone finding out about their trips to Steorra. If they were found out, the magic wouldn't work anymore and they'd never be able to get back to the magical land.

"I probably just put it in the wrong place on my bookshelf," Amelia said. She didn't seem worried as she swung her backpack off her shoulder and pulled out a small package wrapped in blue paper and tied with ribbon.

"I should have got Pascal a present too," Ethan said.

"I wrote your name on the tag," Amelia said. "It's from us both."

"It's not really though," Ethan said as he trudged up the stairs. "You thought of it *and* made it."

"It doesn't matter," Amelia said. "Pascal won't care that you didn't bring him anything. Friendship isn't about *things*. It's just about being friends."

Deep down Ethan thought Amelia was probably right. But he still wished he had a present for Pascal. He'd spent all week trying to think of something but the only idea he had was a new fishing rod and he didn't have any money for it.

Pascal hated the water so he used a fishing rod instead of swimming for fish like the other penguins. Ethan wasn't sure why he wouldn't swim. Perhaps he could find out. If he could help Pascal overcome his fear of the water he wouldn't even need a new fishing rod!

"Are we going?" Amelia asked, holding the orange dragon on her hand.

"Yes." Ethan took the green dragon from the box, then paused.

The thought of going back to Steorra made him forget all of his worries. Every time they visited was always such a great adventure.

When he looked at Amelia she was smiling so brightly that he couldn't help but do the same. He watched her fingers curl around the orange dragon. At the same time he squeezed the green dragon. Closing his eyes was automatic.

When he opened them again, he was on the back of Enzo. He was used to the feel of the dragon's scales now and found them comforting. The wind rushed through his hair and he was filled with excitement.

The rumble of Enzo's laugh was wonderfully familiar. Beside him, Amelia rode on Erla, the orange dragon, and cried out excitedly. It made Ethan laugh. Then he threw an arm up in the air and gave a whoop of joy.

The dragons raced through the clouds,

bursting through them into a bright blue sky.
When they slowed over the forest, Ethan gazed
below until he spotted the landing site at the
same time as Amelia. They both cried out at
once.

"Pascal will be so happy to see you," Erla said when they were down on solid ground.

"Has the party started yet?" Amelia asked.

"No," Enzo said, stepping away from the delicate flowers which made up the landing spot. The small yellow blooms had been flattened by the dragons but popped straight up again when they moved away. "The party is this afternoon. But Pascal's in a terrible mood."

"Why?" Ethan asked. "It's his birthday. No one can be in a bad mood on their birthday."

"They can when Jojo is around," Enzo said, then set off tramping through the forest.

"What's she done now?" Amelia asked. They'd met the mischievous fairy before. She liked to play tricks on people and could be very mean.

"She stole all the fairy dust," Erla said. "So now they can't play bubble burst at the party."

"What's bubble burst?" Amelia asked.

"A party game," Enzo said. "The penguins make bubbles with fairy dust and send them into the air. Whoever bursts the most bubbles is the winner."

"It's difficult," Erla told them. "Because the fairy dust makes the bubbles hard to break, and they whizz around quickly."

"That sounds like so much fun," Amelia said, striding along between the dragons. "Why did Jojo take her fairy dust back?"

"It wasn't her dust," Enzo said. "It comes from the other fairies."

"There are more fairies?" Ethan asked in surprise.

Erla nodded her long scaly head. "The other fairies stay in the fairy cave. They don't like to come out much, but every so often they leave fairy dust at the cave entrance. The pixies collect it and share it around."

"Can't the pixies go and get some more?" Amelia said.

Enzo turned to her. "They tried but there isn't any outside the cave and they're scared to go in and ask. The fairies don't like anyone going into the cave."

"We could go," Amelia said. "I'd love to go into a fairy cave."

"I wouldn't," Ethan said. "Not if the fairies are as mean as Jojo."

"The other fairies aren't usually mean," Erla said. "As long as no one goes into their cave anyway."

Amelia beamed at Ethan. "We're going to get

the fairy dust for Pascal. Then we'll play bubble burst at his party."

Ethan wasn't as excited as Amelia was about disturbing the fairies.

But if he helped get the fairy dust it might make up for not having a present for Pascal.

Ethan always loved the sight of Pascal's house when they emerged from the forest. It made him smile to see the wonderfully wintery scene in the middle of the otherwise grassy field.

The stars overhead twinkled brightly in every colour of the rainbow. They reflected onto the ice and snow around Pascal's house. Today, everything looked brighter than ever. Even the icicles which hung from the roof glistened.

The dragons stayed back so their warm breath didn't melt Pascal's house while Ethan and Amelia slipped and stumbled across the ice to greet Pascal.

"I'm so glad you're here," Pascal said, waddling out to meet them and pushing his glasses onto his beak. "I thought you might have an idea for another game if we can't play bubble burst."

"We're going to play it!" Amelia said firmly. "Ethan and I are going to the fairy cave to get the fairy dust for you."

Pascal hopped from foot to foot. It made him look like he was dancing and Ethan couldn't help but laugh.

"Happy Birthday!" Ethan said.

"Oh, yes, Happy Birthday," Amelia said, holding out her gift. "We brought you a present."

"You shouldn't have," Pascal said. "But thank you." He couldn't quite manage to unwrap it with his flippers so Amelia stepped forward to help him. He gave an excited squeak when he saw the hat and scarf. Ethan helped him to put them on and they all said how great he looked.

"We'll need to go straight to the cave," Enzo said. "Otherwise we won't make it back before the party."

"Yes," Pascal agreed. "We'll go now. I do hope the fairies will give you more fairy dust."

"Where's Jojo?" Ethan asked as they set off across the field.

"Hiding," Pascal said. "She knows everyone

is cross with her for taking the fairy dust so she'll stay away for a while."

When they reached the edge of the field, Pascal flopped onto his tummy and set off sliding down the hill towards the village. Ethan and Amelia climbed into a hollowed-out tree trunk and whizzed down as though they were on a log flume without the water. They were both laughing when they reached the bottom. Ethan couldn't imagine a more fun way to get down the hill.

For a moment, Ethan paused to look at the village. Ice houses sparkled under the light of the glittering stars. The wonderful sky reflected on the surface of the lake and the starlight seemed to dance on the ripples of the water. It was the most beautiful place Ethan had ever seen.

As his group of friends set off through the village, Ethan hurried to catch them up. They walked quickly, saying hello to everyone they passed. The goblins looked a little grumpy, as usual, but the polar bears and penguins were friendly and smiled at the children.

Soon, they reached the other side of the village. From there, a snow-covered path snaked up the mountain. Neither Ethan nor Amelia had ever ventured that far before. The furthest they'd been was the village by the lake.

"How far away is the cave?" Amelia asked.

"Not far," Enzo said. "Just up on the first ridge."

Ethan paused and looked ahead. The path wound its way steadily up, then levelled off for a while. He thought he could make out the dark entrance to a cave. It wouldn't take them long to reach it. Which meant that very soon he'd have to venture into a cave in the mountainside. He wished that Amelia wasn't always so brave and adventurous.

He trudged along the path with his little group of friends. Before he knew it, they were standing on the wide ridge which ran around the side of the mountain.

"This is so exciting," Amelia announced at the entrance to the cave.

"It's dark," Ethan pointed out. "How are we going to see where we're going?"

Pascal peered into the cave. "Once you get around the first bend, you'll see the light from the fairies."

"You've been in there?" Ethan asked.

"Yes. When I was a curious little penguin."

Ethan peeked into the dark cave then looked back at Pascal. "So you could come with us and show us the way?"

"Oh no," Pascal said. "The fairies shouted at me. They told me never to come back again."

"Come on," Amelia said, tugging on Ethan's sleeve.

"But they're going to be angry with us," Ethan protested. He really wanted to help get the fairy dust for Pascal, but he was nervous too. "Couldn't we try shouting to them?" he asked.

"They might come out and then we could ask them for the fairy dust."

"Where's the fun in that?" Amelia asked. "This is probably my only chance to see a fairy cave. I'm not going to miss it."

Ethan opened his mouth to speak, but Amelia took a step into the cave. Then another. And another. Before he could say anything, Amelia had disappeared from sight.

Ethan swallowed hard, thinking again about not having a birthday present for Pascal.

He'd be brave and help to get the fairy dust instead.

Taking a deep breath, he stepped into the cave.

CHAPTER SIX
INTO THE CAVE

The walls were cold and damp as Ethan felt his way into the cave. His heart was beating furiously and part of him wanted to run back outside.

"Look," Amelia whispered, standing just ahead of him. She held her arm out, pointing to a faint glow of light coming from deeper inside the mountain.

"I'm scared," Ethan said.

"Me too." Amelia reached out and took his hand. "But it's exciting as well."

It was comforting to hear that Amelia was scared too, even if she didn't really seem it. Together they crept further into the cave.

Amelia gasped when they walked around the

next corner. It wasn't dark anymore. The walls glowed with hundreds of tiny lights.

Ethan kept hold of Amelia's hand as they tiptoed along. When his eyes adjusted to the light he could hardly believe what he saw. Along the wall were holes in the rock. Like small caves within the cave. Each hole was a tiny glowing house. The one in front of them had a tiny wooden bed with a blanket made from a pink flower petal. A green leaf lay on the floor for a carpet.

"That's amazing," Amelia said, her voice so faint it was hard to hear.

They moved silently along the wall, peering into the dainty houses. One had a small table and chair made from tiny twigs and bits of plants. The next had walls painted with a picture of a rainbow and multi-coloured stars. Then, they came to one with a purple petal laying atop the bed. There was a table beside the bed and a fairy stood arranging bluebells in a vase. She had her back to Ethan and Amelia so she didn't notice them watching her.

Ethan squeezed Amelia's hand tightly. He hardly dared to move or even breathe. Any moment now the fairy would turn and see them.

Then they'd find out how mean the fairies really were.

"Hello," Amelia said, breaking the silence with her shaky voice.

Slowly, the fairy turned and squinted at them. Ethan thought she would have been startled, or even scared by them. But she seemed very calm as she stepped to the edge of her cave. She wore jeans and a yellow T-shirt with her wings sticking out behind her. At first she looked them both up and down. Then she screwed her face up and put her hand on her hips.

"Pixies!" she shouted at what appeared to be the top of her lungs. It wasn't really very loud but she definitely looked cross.

"We're not pixies," Amelia said quickly.

The fairy's head twitched to look at Amelia. Her little face turned red and she took a deep breath before opening her mouth wide. "Pixies!" she shouted again. This time her voice seemed to bounce off the walls and echo all around them.

When the echo died out, Ethan felt a gentle breeze at his neck and heard a low buzzing sound.

"What's that?" he asked, looking frantically at Amelia. The buzzing grew louder until Ethan had to put his hands over his ears.

"Fairies," Amelia said, turning in a circle. "*Lots* of fairies."

The buzzing sound was hundreds of pairs of wings fluttering at the same time. Ethan turned around to see the air alive with fairies. A whole crowd of them hung in the space around the children. They were all dressed in jeans and brightly coloured T-shirts. None of them looked happy to have visitors.

"Pixies aren't allowed in our caves," one of them called, flying closer to them.

"We're not p-pixies," Ethan stuttered as the noise of the wings died down.

"What are you then?" the fairy asked, whizzing forwards to inspect them more closely.

"People," Amelia said. "Humans."

Another fairy darted at Ethan, whizzing

around the side of his head. "Look at their ears," she said. "They're definitely not pixies."

"You're not from Steorra, are you?" the one in front of Amelia said.

"No," she replied. "We just came for a visit."

"We don't like visitors," a small voice called from the crowd.

"We came to visit Pascal," Amelia explained. "He's a penguin. It's his birthday and he's having a party. He was going to play a game with floating bubbles but he needs fairy dust and Jojo stole it all."

There was a lot of grumbling and shaking of heads.

"Jojo's always up to no good," a fairy in a blue T-shirt told them. "She thinks we're boring so she doesn't come into the cave very often."

"We wanted to ask if you could give us more fairy dust," Amelia said. "If you've got any?"

That sent a ripple of laughter around the fairies.

"We're fairies," the one near Amelia said. "Of course we've got fairy dust."

"Could we have some?" Ethan asked. He wasn't feeling quite as scared but he still wanted to get out of the cave as quickly as possible.

"We don't like anyone coming into the cave,"

the fairy in front of Ethan said, scrunching her face up. She looked angry and even though she was tiny, Ethan felt a bit scared of her.

"What's your name?" Amelia asked the fairy.

"Lulu," she said huffily.

Amelia and Ethan introduced themselves and a few other fairies told them their names too. The one nearest to Amelia was called Clea and behind her were Fifi, Gina, and Beck.

"Why don't you like anyone coming into your cave?" Amelia asked. "You don't seem mean like Jojo."

Lulu's face relaxed and she didn't look as cross. "We like peace and quiet, that's all. The goblins and pixies stamp around and make everything shake. And penguins make a lot of noise with their shuffling feet."

"I understand that," Amelia said with a wide smile. "Sometimes my house is too noisy as well."

"We're not mean," Lulu said. "We know everyone likes our fairy dust so we leave it outside the cave."

"Please could we have some for Pascal's party?" Ethan asked again. "It would make him really happy."

"Okay then," Lulu said after a moment. "Follow me." She flew further into the cave. The crowd of fairies moved apart but followed when Amelia and Ethan set off after Lulu.

"Where does the fairy dust come from?" Amelia asked. "Do you make it?"

Clea flew between them. "No. It just appears. Every few days we sweep up the floor in our houses and there it is!"

"Like normal dust," Amelia said, grinning.

"My mum is always complaining about dust. At least your dust is magic."

"What use is dust if it isn't magic?" Clea asked.

"There is no use," Amelia said. "That's why it's so annoying."

"Well, ours is magic," Lulu said, slowing down and fluttering beside the wall. "And we have lots of it!"

Ethan stopped and stared at the section of wall beside them.

He could hardly believe his eyes.

CHAPTER EIGHT
FAIRY DUST

On the wall were lots and lots of long shelves. Sitting neatly on the shelves were hundreds of tiny glass bottles. Ethan couldn't see what was in the bottles because they twinkled so brightly that it hurt his eyes and he had to look away. But even though he couldn't see it he knew without a doubt that it was fairy dust.

"There's so much!" Amelia said. "What do you do with it?"

"Mostly we used it for light," Lulu said. "We sprinkle it on the walls to make them glow."

"We don't need it all," Clea said. "So we give some to the pixies and they share it out in the village. They usually use it to make things fly."

"It's beautiful," Amelia said. Ethan nodded his head in agreement. It was certainly much nicer than the dust which collected in his house.

Four fairies flew over to the shelf, each holding the corner of a piece of grey material. Lulu and Clea swooped up to the shelf and began picking up bottles and laying them on the material. Once they had about twenty bottles, the four fairies flew together, bringing the corners of the material together to make a bag. Two more fairies flew around with a length of string, tying it so that the bottles were secured inside.

"That should be plenty," Lulu said, as the fairies flew over to Ethan and held out the bag to him.

"Thank you," he said as he took it from them.

Clea flew in front of Ethan and did a little twirl in the air. "The penguin will know what to do with it," she said with a twinkle in her eyes. "It's very easy; you just sprinkle it on whatever you want to make fly and off it will go."

"I can't wait to see Pascal's face when we bring him the fairy dust," Ethan said, smiling gratefully at Clea who remained hovering close to his face.

Beside him Amelia's eyes gazed all around as though she was trying to memorise every detail of the fairy cave. "I can't wait to play bubble burst at the birthday party," she said.

"That does sound like a lot of fun," Clea said. With a gentle laugh she held out her hand and held it flatly in front of her face. Then she blew out a long stream of breath.

As tiny particles rained over Ethan, he

coughed and spluttered. "What was that for?" he asked.

Clea didn't reply but held her stomach while she laughed. The other fairies crowded around. All of them were laughing.

"What's so funny?" Ethan asked. He didn't like the way they were all looking at him and laughing.

"Ethan!" Amelia gasped. "You're getting taller!"

He looked beside him to find that Amelia seemed to be getting smaller. It took him a moment to realise what was really happening.

"I'm not growing," he said, shaking his legs furiously. "I'm flying!"

CHAPTER NINE
FLYING

E than couldn't stop kicking his legs. It only made him float upwards more quickly.

"Help!" he shouted, then felt Amelia's hand grab at his leg.

"What did you do?" she shouted at Clea.

"It's just a bit of fun," she giggled. "I thought he'd like to try flying."

"I can't keep hold of you," Amelia said, clinging desperately to his shoe.

Lulu flew in front of Amelia's face, grinning at her. "I can help with that," she said before throwing a handful of dust over her head.

Amelia rose up off the ground as Ethan had. "I'm flying too," she shrieked.

"Looks more like floating to me," Clea said.

"And if you don't stop soon you'll bang your head on the roof of the cave."

Ethan looked up to see the rough stone ceiling above him. At least he couldn't go very far. He put his hands out when he reached it so he didn't bump his head.

"You're mean," he shouted. "Just like Jojo!"

"We're not mean," Lulu said crossly as she flew up beside him. "We thought you'd enjoy having a bit of a fly around. And the magic won't last forever. Just a little while."

"What happens when it wears off?" Ethan asked. Even though the ceiling wasn't very high, he didn't like the thought of falling to the ground. "Will I crash back down?"

"No!" Clea said. "You'll float down, the same as you floated up. We'd never let you get hurt."

"It is quite good fun," Amelia said as she floated up beside him.

"Push off from the ceiling and have a fly around," Lulu said. "Then you'll really enjoy yourselves."

"How?" Amelia asked. "All we do is go up. And we're as high as we can go."

"Use your arms and legs," Clea said. "Pretend you're swimming."

Ethan frowned at Amelia. "I think it's best to stay here until the magic wears off."

He should have known better than to think Amelia would listen. A wide smile stretched over her face and she pushed off from the ceiling.

She gave a high-pitched squeal as she jetted downwards before slowing and hovering in mid-air. Laughing, she moved her arms up and down, testing which way she went. Then she dived forwards and did a somersault.

"Come on!" she shouted to Ethan. "It's fantastic. You have to try it."

After watching Amelia for a moment, he gave a gentle push off and floated down to her.

"Use your arms," she said, waving her hands up and down.

Ethan tried it and found that he could easily control moving around. After a few minutes he felt much more confident. He was having a brilliant time.

"How long will it last?" Amelia asked, giggling as she flew with the fairies.

"Probably not much longer," Clea said. "It's hard to say."

"Pascal and the dragons are waiting for us," Ethan said. He would be very happy to spend all day flying around the fairy cave, but they needed to leave in time for Pascal's party. "We were supposed to be quick."

"Can we fly out?" Amelia asked.

"Certainly," Lulu said. "We'll come with you."

Together Ethan and Amelia flew with the fairies towards the mouth of the cave.

"Thank you so much," Amelia called, when the fairies stopped.

"You're welcome," Lulu said as the crowd of fairies waved. "Enjoy the party."

"We will," Ethan replied, smiling back at the fairies and raising a hand to wave.

"Oh, my goodness!" Pascal said in a squeaky voice as he caught sight of them. "What happened?"

"They covered us in fairy dust," Amelia said. "Now we can fly!"

"It will wear off soon," Ethan assured Pascal. "And we have the fairy dust for the party," he said, holding up the bag.

"Thank you," Pascal said. "I'm so excited about the party. I just hope Jojo stays away and doesn't do anything else to ruin it."

CHAPTER TEN
DOWN THE MOUNTAIN

The journey down the mountain was much more fun than on the way up. Amelia and Ethan had a wonderful time flying around the dragon's heads. Everyone was laughing, and the time went fast. They were just reaching the village when Ethan's legs felt suddenly heavy and he sank down to the ground.

"Oh no!" Amelia cried when she landed beside him a moment later. "Flying is the best thing ever. Could we use some of the fairy dust so we can fly all the way back to Pascal's house?"

"We need it for the game," Pascal said. "I don't want to use it all up."

"Can we fly for the game?" Amelia asked.

"No," Pascal said with a laugh. "The bubbles fly, not the players."

"Don't the bubbles float away?" Ethan asked.

"No." Pascal looked thoughtful, as though it had never occurred to him that they might. "They just bounce around, even if they go high, they come back down again eventually."

"I can't wait," Amelia said, quickening her pace.

"I wish there was time for a snack," Pascal said to Ethan as they walked together behind the others. "I was so worried about the party this morning that I didn't have any breakfast."

"Don't we have time before the party?" Ethan asked.

"No, because I'd have to go home and get my fishing rod first." Pascal gazed sadly out across the lake where some of the other penguins were swimming. "If only I could dive in and catch fish like the other penguins."

"Why don't you like to swim?" Ethan asked, remembering his idea to help Pascal to get into the water. "Don't you know how?"

"I used to be a very good swimmer," he said proudly. "But I had a bit of a problem when I was younger and I've never been back in the water since."

"What kind of problem?" Ethan asked.

"I was swimming and another penguin didn't see me. He dived in and bumped me on the head."

"Ouch," Ethan said.

"Yes, it hurt a lot."

"And you never went in the water again?" Ethan asked. "You didn't even try?"

Pascal shook his head. "I was too scared.

"That's a shame," Ethan said. He paused and looked at all the other penguins splashing around in the water. He didn't think he'd be able to persuade Pascal to swim, but he wanted to give it a go. "Maybe you could try swimming again," he said.

"I couldn't. Even thinking about getting in the water scares me."

Ethan smiled at Pascal. "I understand. I'm scared of lots of things."

"Like what?" Pascal asked, stopping on the path and looking up at Ethan.

"The first time I flew on Enzo I was terrified. And the first time I went down the hill in the tree trunk I was scared too."

Pascal's beak twitched. "Really?"

"Yes. Today I was afraid to go in the fairy cave. And when the fairy threw her dust on me I didn't want to try and fly."

"But you did it anyway?" Pascal asked.

"Yes. And I had a great time. Sometimes it's good to try things, even if it scares you. If you hate it you don't have to do it again. But there are some things that just seem scary until you try them."

"So you think I should try swimming again?" Ethan's eyes darted to the water. "Yes."

"I don't know," Pascal said, his beak twitching nervously.

"I think you'll be fine if you give it a try," Ethan said, trying to encourage Pascal.

"I can't," Pascal said. "I'm not brave enough."

"Maybe later," Ethan said sadly, wishing for a way to help Pascal face his fear.

"We'll be coming to the lake after the party for a fish dinner," Pascal said. "The other penguins were going to catch them for me because it's my birthday, but maybe I can have a go at swimming then. I'll think about it."

They carried on walking and had just caught up to Amelia and the dragons when someone called out to Pascal. It was Maxwell, a polar bear who they'd met before. He was surrounded by a small crowd of penguins.

"Happy Birthday!" Maxwell called. "We're coming for the party. Are we too early?"

"No," Pascal replied. "Perfect timing. We had to go to the fairy caves to get more fairy dust. Now we're all set for a game of bubble burst."

"Can we play penguin bowl too?" one of the smaller penguins asked.

Ethan and Amelia stared at each other, both wondering the same thing...

What on earth was penguin bowl?

CHAPTER ELEVEN
PENGUIN BOWLING

"What's penguin bowl?" Ethan asked, as the group walked together towards the hill.

"You have bowling in your land, don't you?" Pascal asked.

"Yes," Ethan replied.

"Well, it's bowling with penguins."

"What do you use for the skittles?" Amelia asked.

"Penguins!" Pascal said, smiling brightly.

Ethan laughed. "What about the bowling ball?"

"Penguins!" Pascal said again. "Although I suppose you could have a go too."

Ethan looked at Amelia and they both

laughed. It sounded as though the game was throwing penguins at penguins, which seemed quite dangerous.

When they reached the moving staircase at the side of the hill, Ethan was so excited about the party that he forgot to be nervous on the fast-moving escalator.

Once everyone had made it to the top of the hill, they walked to the patch of snow behind Pascal's house. The dragons wandered to the grass nearby and lay down for a rest.

"Maxwell!" Pascal called. "Would you mind clearing a lane for us?"

"Not at all," the polar bear replied in his deep voice. "Stand aside everyone." Maxwell walked a little away from them before turning and running very fast across the snow. When he was at full speed, he pushed his front paws forwards and dropped onto his belly. Snow flew all around as he skidded, leaving a smooth patch of hard snow behind him.

"That's the bowling lane," Pascal told the children. "I get to go first because it's my birthday."

The children watched as the other penguins waddled along the icy bowling lane. When they reached the end they lined themselves up in rows, just like the skittles on a bowling lane.

Ethan still wasn't sure what was going to happen. He was worried about the penguins getting hurt but they all looked very jolly.

Before he knew it, Pascal moved back for a run up then set off as fast as he could towards the bowling lane. When he reached it he lurched onto his tummy and gave himself a push with his flippers. He whizzed towards the penguins. Ethan could hardly bear to watch, sure that one of them was going to get hurt.

Laughter rang all around as Pascal collided with the penguins and sent all except one of them crashing to the ground.

"Doesn't it hurt?" Amelia asked as they walked closer to the penguins.

"No. We're quite rubbery!" one of the penguins said, wriggling his way out of the soft snow he'd fallen into.

"Would you like a turn?" Pascal asked.

"Yes!" Amelia cried, then ran to the starting point. She waited while the penguins got themselves back into place. After a short sprint she propelled herself onto her stomach and cried out in delight as she whizzed towards the penguins. She slowed slightly before she reached them and veered a little to the left so she only knocked two of them over.

"It takes some practice to get your aim right," Pascal said as Amelia stood up and dusted snow off her clothes.

"Your turn!" she said to Ethan.

It was difficult to run through the snow, but Ethan moved as fast as he could before diving onto his tummy. Cold pieces of snow flicked up into his face making it difficult to see whether he was on target or not.

He'd just begun to slow down when he hit a penguin with a dull thud. The penguins were indeed quite rubbery. Hitting them didn't hurt at all.

Ethan looked around to see them lying on the ground. Only one penguin was still upright and he wobbled precariously from side to side. He made a clicking sound with his beak before falling over backwards.

Realising he'd knocked all of the penguins over, Ethan jumped up, grinning.

Amelia, Pascal and Maxwell all cheered. Even the dragons called out from across the field. Ethan felt so happy he couldn't stop smiling. He and Amelia moved to help the penguins up, then stood back to watch while they all took turns to have a go.

"I think it's time for cake," Pascal said, when the game came to an end. They followed him to the front of the house, then waited while he went inside.

"I wonder what kind of cake it is," Amelia said to Ethan. "I'm imagining a chocolate cake but I'm worried it might be a cake made from fish."

"Yuk!" Ethan said, pulling a face. "I hope not."

Beside them, Maxwell chuckled. "Don't worry," he said. "I've never seen a cake made from fish. Though it does sound delicious."

A moment later Pascal came back outside. The other penguins shuffled closer to him, flapping excitedly.

On the tray in Pascal's flippers was a huge mound of sparkling white snow.

"That's a cake?" Ethan asked, confused. It didn't look like a cake.

"It's mountain cake," Pascal said proudly as he set the tray down.

Amelia's eyes lit up. "Is it like the mountain flakes we ate at the festival of falling stars?"

"Yes!" Pascal said. "It's made from the same snowflakes from the top of the mountain. But this time I've whipped them up to make ice-cream cake."

One of the smaller penguins stuck a flipper into the cake and took a piece. "It's creamy in the middle," he said, holding it out to show Amelia and Ethan. Beneath the glittery white layer was smooth cream-coloured layer.

"It's the best ice cream you'll ever taste," Pascal told them.

The children dug in with their hands. Thankfully the ice cream wasn't runny like normal ice cream. It felt like holding a firm snowball. When Ethan licked it he found it really was the most delicious ice cream he'd ever tasted. It tingled on his tongue, sweet and delicious.

"That's so much better than a cake made from fish," Amelia said happily.

"I'm going to start getting the bubbles

ready," Pascal announced. "When everyone's finished eating cake we'll play bubble burst."

Ethan looked at Amelia and beamed.

CHAPTER TWELVE
BUBBLE BURST

"Have you played bubble burst before?" Maxwell asked Ethan.

"No," Ethan said while he watched Pascal empty a bottle of fairy dust into a large bowl of soapy water. After tipping three of the bottles in, he took a stick and began to stir.

"It's a great game," Maxwell said.

Ethan peered over Pascal's shoulder, waiting for something to happen. "Shouldn't there be bubbles?" he asked.

"It takes a few minutes," Pascal replied.

"Shall I give it a stir?" Maxwell asked.

Pascal handed him the stick and the polar bear stirred so vigorously that a few drops of water spilled over the edge of the bowl. Finally, a bubble appeared on the surface of the water and grew until it was quite large.

When it floated away, another bubble appeared in the water and then another. As long as Maxwell stirred, the bubbles continued to grow and take off into the air. Ethan tried to count them but it was difficult when they kept moving around. He was sure there were at least a hundred when Maxwell stopped stirring the frothy water.

"Now what do we do?" Amelia asked, craning her neck to look up at the bubbles which hovered high in the air.

"The aim is to burst the bubbles," Pascal said. "Whoever pops the most wins."

"It doesn't really matter who wins though," a smaller penguin said. "It's just fun to pop the bubbles."

"But how can we catch them when they're so high?" Ethan asked.

"Wait a minute," Pascal said, wobbling excitedly from side to side. "Be patient."

The bubbles hung in the air, hardly moving. Ethan wasn't sure what they were waiting for. It didn't seem as though anything was going to happen.

"Here we go," Maxwell said.

"Nothing's happening," Ethan said in confusion. A couple of bubbles drifted a little but that was all.

Pascal hopped up and down. "Keep watching. Any second now."

Finally one bubble bumped into the one beside it. It was just a gentle knock, but it sent the other bubble jolting into the next one. Before long the bubbles were all ping-ponging off each other. Eventually one hit another in such a way that it shot down towards the ground.

Ethan watched as the penguins charged after it. They waddled quickly before pushing on to their tummies and zooming over the snow.

The smallest of the penguins arrived at the bubble just as it reached the ground. His beak drove into it, but the bubble seemed to be made from elastic and only sprang away from him.

Maxwell ran around the penguins to get to the bubble. Ethan was sure he would burst it but it bounced off his huge paw and whooshed upwards again. When it hit the other bubbles, they set off in all directions, many of them whizzing down to the ground.

That time Ethan was determined to pop one. As everyone chased around he managed to grab hold of a smaller bubble. He caught it with two hands then squeezed as hard as he could. Nothing happened. It felt more like a ball than a soap bubble. Pushing it to the ground, he put a foot on it and pushed down with all his weight. The bubble stretched out almost flat, then bounced back to shape and shot away from him.

"It's impossible," he said to Amelia, who did a belly flop onto a bubble only to bounce off again.

"It's fun though," she said, hitting out and sending a bubble flying up into the air.

"Got one!" Pascal called. They turned in time to see the splashes from the burst bubble.

"How did you do that?" Ethan asked.

"It gets easier as the magic wears off," Pascal replied happily.

Laughing, Amelia ran at a bubble and jumped on it with both feet. After hovering on top of it for a moment, there was a pop and Amelia crashed to the ground. "Go one!" she shouted, jumping back up and running across the snow. She leaped on another and shouted that she'd got two.

Ethan felt suddenly competitive and shot into action to pop as many bubbles as he could.

It didn't take him long to forget all about winning. Soon, his cheeks ached from laughing. He couldn't remember ever having so much fun.

But when a familiar fairy flew past him with a mischievous glint in her eye, Ethan had a sinking feeling in his stomach.

He was sure the fun was about to come to an end.

CHAPTER THIRTEEN
JOJO CAUSING TROUBLE

Ethan watched Jojo fly around, bursting the bubbles up high so no one else had a chance.

"Stop that!" Amelia shouted. Her voice was angry and her features were scrunched up as she looked at Jojo. "Stop it right now."

"Please, stop," Pascal cried beside her. "You're ruining the game, Jojo."

"I'm only popping the bubbles like everyone else," Jojo's squeaky voice called back.

"Stop it right now," Amelia shouted angrily.

"Or what?" Jojo asked with a naughty giggle.

"Or I'll come up there and stop you," Amelia replied, going red in the face. "It's Pascal's birthday and I won't let you ruin it."

"You can't get up here," Jojo said, poking another bubble.

"I could get the fairy dust!" Amelia said. "Then I could fly up there and stop you. Or you could stop being mean and do something useful for once."

Jojo stopped bursting bubbles and drifted closer to Amelia. "Like what?" she asked.

"You could keep score," Amelia said.

"That sounds boring." Jojo started to fly away again, but Amelia called after her.

"Can't you manage it?" she asked. "Have you been too busy being mean that you didn't learn to count?"

"Of course I can count," Jojo huffed. "And I'd do a brilliant job because I have the best view from up here."

"I don't think you can do it," Amelia said, turning away from Jojo and flashing Ethan a quick smile.

"I can!" Jojo shouted. She reached under her wing and pulled out a tiny scroll of paper. "You carry on playing and I'll prove I can keep score."

"I've popped ten bubbles so far," Amelia said, then turned to Ethan. "How many have you got?"

"Eight, I think." He jumped up to catch another while Jojo scribbled away on her paper. "Nine now!"

"I've got twelve," Maxwell told Jojo, then bounded away after a bubble.

Now that Jojo had a job to do she stopped causing trouble and everyone got back to the game. Amelia and Ethan had a brilliant time. When the last bubble burst, Ethan was tired from so much running, and so much laughing.

"Who won?" Amelia asked Jojo.

The fairy flew down and hovered beside

Pascal. "Everyone did very well," she said, seeming proud of her role in the game. "But Pascal is the winner!"

Everyone cheered and Pascal looked very pleased with himself.

"Thanks for keeping score," he said to Jojo.

"You're welcome," she said. Her cheeks turned pink. "I'm sorry for trying to spoil the game. Happy Birthday!" she called before flying quickly away.

Pascal stared after her. "I've never known Jojo to say sorry for anything before," he said, then gave a quick shake of his head.

Ethan wondered if Jojo was so naughty because no one let her join their games. When Amelia had invited her to join them she'd stopped being unkind.

"Bubble burst is the best game I've ever played," Amelia said. "Can we play again?"

"I'm getting hungry," Pascal said. "I think it's time to go down to the lake and eat some fish."

Maxwell and the penguins agreed that they were hungry too. The dragons joined them as everyone set off towards the hill. It was fun to watch all the penguins whizzing down on their tummies. Maxwell laughed as he glided down beside Ethan and Amelia when they climbed into the tree trunk.

At the bottom of the hill Ethan left Amelia and ran over to Pascal.

"Are you going to try swimming?" he asked quietly as they walked a little away from the rest of the group.

"I don't think I want to," Pascal said, wobbling as he walked. "I've had a lovely birthday and I don't want to ruin it. It was a fun party, wasn't it? Thank goodness Amelia stood up to Jojo and didn't let her ruin the party."

"Amelia's always brave," Ethan said. "When the kids on our street are mean, she always stands up to them. I wish I could."

"I'm sure you could if you tried," Pascal said.

Ethan shook his head. "When they tease me I always want to say something to them but I get too scared and my mind goes blank."

"Next time just tell them not to be mean," Pascal said.

"Maybe," Ethan said. It sounded so easy now, but when they were in front of him it wasn't easy at all. "I know!" Ethan said, stopping beside the lake. "I'll promise to try and stand up to the mean kids, if you give swimming a try. We'll both be brave."

"Will you really do it?" Pascal asked, looking nervously at the water.

"I promise!" he said. "If you swim."

"I don't know if I can," Pascal said.

Ethan put a hand on the penguin's flipper. "If you think about it too much, you'll get more scared. The best thing to do is take a deep breath and jump in."

Pascal blinked a few times before he took off his hat and scarf and gave them to Ethan. Then he waddled closer to the water's edge. There was a squeak before he dived.

Shocked, Ethan stood looking at the ripples on the water where Pascal had disappeared. He was surprised that Pascal had taken his advice. Suddenly, Ethan worried about his little penguin friend. What if he'd forgotten how to swim? Or what if he got another bump on his head?

As he stared at the water, Ethan forgot to breathe.

There was no sign of Pascal anywhere.

"What happened?" Amelia asked, slightly out of breath as she ran over to Ethan.

"P-Pascal … he … he's gone," Ethan stuttered.

Enzo padded over and stood beside Ethan "Gone where?" he asked.

"He dived in," Ethan said, his eyes searching for any sign of Pascal.

"Into the water?" Erla asked in disbelief. "He's scared of swimming."

"I know." Ethan's heart was beating like crazy and he felt terrible for encouraging Pascal. "I told him not to be afraid and to give it a try."

"He's been gone for so long," Amelia said. "Should someone go in after him?"

"Penguins can hold their breath for a long

time," Enzo said. "And the water here is different to the water in your world. Nothing bad can happen, he'll pop up again in a minute."

Ethan couldn't help but worry as they waited. Time seemed to slow down. Then all of a sudden there was a splash and Pascal's head popped out of the water.

"I shouldn't have done that," he called.

"I'm sorry," Ethan said as Pascal swam closer to them. "I thought it might be good for you."

Pascal beamed at him. "It was brilliant! I'd forgotten how much I loved to swim."

"What's the problem then?" Enzo asked. A puff of smoke escaped his nostrils as he chuckled.

"I didn't take my glasses off. They fell off and I had to swim around after them. Could you take them?" he asked Ethan.

Ethan stepped to the edge of the water and took the glasses and their chain from around Pascal's neck.

"I'll be back in a minute," Pascal said. "This time I'm going fishing!" He gave a squeaky laugh and disappeared under the water again.

"I can't believe you got him to swim," Erla said as she lay down beside the lake. "We've been trying to get him to swim for years but he was always too scared."

"Well done," Amelia said, bumping her shoulder against Ethan's.

"I didn't really do anything." Ethan felt his cheeks warming up and hoped they weren't bright red. He watched as Maxwell and the penguins jumped and dived into the lake with

Pascal. It was hard to tell the penguins apart in the water. Ethan thought he saw Pascal a couple of times but he dived under the water again before Ethan could get a proper look.

It was about five minutes later when he popped up in front of them.

"Six fish!" he cried. "I ate six fish. I'm stuffed. I haven't eaten so much in years!"

"That's what you're supposed to do on your birthday," Amelia said. "Eat your favourite food until you feel like you might burst."

Pascal gave a happy sigh. "I definitely feel full enough to burst. And I think this has been the best birthday I've ever had."

"I was a bit worried when it took you so long to come out of the water," Ethan said while he helped Pascal put his hat and scarf on again.

"Jumping in was scary," Pascal admitted. "But as soon as I was in the water I was fine. I should have done it years ago. I'm going to go swimming every day from now on."

"I'm afraid it's time to go home," Enzo said to the children.

Amelia frowned. "I wish we could stay longer."

"I had such a brilliant day," Ethan said to Pascal. "Thank you for inviting us."

"Thank you for my hat and scarf," Pascal said.

"You're welcome," Amelia replied.

Pascal turned to look at Ethan. "And thank you for giving me the courage to go swimming. That's the best gift I could have wished for."

"Really?" Ethan asked.

"Yes. I can't wait to go swimming tomorrow. I can throw away my fishing rod! But don't forget what you promised me in return."

"I won't," Ethan replied.

They said goodbye to Pascal and waved to Maxwell and the other penguins before setting off with the dragons.

"What did Pascal mean about you promising him something?" Amelia asked Ethan while they walked.

Ethan sighed. "I told him how I'm always scared to say anything to the boys from our street when they tease me. I promised I'd try and stand up to them if he tried swimming."

"You can definitely do that," Amelia said.

Ethan wasn't so sure. He was happy that Pascal had found the courage to swim, but he still didn't think he was brave enough to stand up for himself.

CHAPTER FIFTEEN
BIKE RIDING

When they arrived back in Ethan's room there was a loud banging coming from the front door.

"Who's that?" Amelia asked, while Ethan hurried to the stairs and thundered down them. He was terrified of getting caught out when they were on one of their trips to Steorra.

Before he answered the door, Ethan darted into the living room and looked through the window to see who it was.

"It's your mum," he told Amelia as he went back into the hallway.

"I hope she hasn't been looking for us," Amelia said.

"What if she found your invitation to Pascal's party and wants to know what it's about?"

"I don't think so," Amelia said as Ethan moved nervously to open the door.

"Didn't you hear me?" Mrs Hopton asked.

"We were upstairs playing a game," Amelia said.

"Well, I was just thinking it would be a good idea for you to go outside and play. Have you been cooped up inside all day?"

"We were out for a little while," Amelia said, stifling a smile as she caught Ethan's eye. "In the back garden."

"It's lovely and sunny," Mrs Hopton said. "There's half an hour before dinner. Why don't you go for a quick bike ride?"

"Do you want to?" Amelia asked Ethan.

"Okay," he replied. "I can't go far though in case my dad comes back and wonders where I am."

"Just play in front of the house," Amelia's mum said. "But get out and get some fresh air, please."

They walked together to Amelia's house. Her mum went inside and Amelia and Ethan went straight into the garage to get the bikes.

"Weren't you worried about your mum finding the invitation?" Ethan asked.

Amelia shook her head. "If she finds it I'll tell

her we made it ourselves for a game."

"What if she doesn't believe you?" Ethan asked.

"Then I'd tell her the truth."

"What?" Ethan was shocked. "You wouldn't really, would you?"

"It wouldn't matter if I did," Amelia told him. "If I tell her we flew on dragons to go to a penguin's birthday party, she'd pat me on the head and tell me I have a lovely imagination."

Ethan chuckled. He hadn't thought about it like that.

"You worry too much," Amelia said.

Ethan borrowed the BMX again. He walked it down the drive while Amelia searched for her helmet.

Some of the other boys had made a ramp in the road and were taking it in turns to ride their bikes over it.

"Do you want a turn?" Zac asked, riding over to Ethan. "I bet your bike will jump really well."

"Erm ..." Ethan wasn't sure. Riding over the ramp looked like fun. It was the first time any of the kids had asked him to play. It made him feel good to be invited but he wasn't sure if he should.

"Are you having a go or what?" Freddie shouted from the road. His eyes flicked behind Ethan. "Hey, vampire! No blood suckers allowed on the ramp."

Sadness flashed in Amelia's eyes before her mouth set into a frown. "I'd never play with you anyway," she snapped.

Seeing Amelia upset made Ethan angry. It wasn't fair that they teased her. He thought about Jojo always being mean in Steorra, and how Amelia had stopped her when she'd tried to ruin Pascal's party. Then he remembered his promise to Pascal. He'd promised to stick up for himself, but he wanted to stick up for Amelia too.

"Are you coming?" Freddie asked Ethan.

"You're mean," he replied quietly.

Freddie rode his bike closer to Ethan. "What did you say?"

Taking a deep breath, Ethan looked straight at Freddie. "I said you're mean. Amelia didn't do anything to you."

"So you'd rather play with her?"

Ethan glanced at the other boys who laughed and cheered as they went over the bike ramp.

"Yes," he said firmly. "She's more fun than you. And she's never mean." His heart was

beating furiously but he forced himself to hold
Freddie's gaze.

"We didn't want to play with you anyway,"
Freddie said. "Have fun with your girlfriend."

Ethan knew he was just trying to annoy him
and he wasn't going to let him.

As Freddie and Zac rode back to join the other kids, Ethan set off in the other direction.

"Thanks," Amelia said as she rode beside him. "I knew you could stand up to them."

Ethan had surprised himself. He'd never thought he could say anything back to them. But it felt good.

"It's true what I told them," he said to Amelia. "I'd much rather play with you. And they definitely don't have as much fun as we do."

"You're right about that!" Amelia agreed with a laugh.

ABOUT THE AUTHOR

Hannah spent most of her career working with children, both in nursery schools and as a nanny for families in various parts of the world.

Feeling like a change, she began writing and publishing books for grown-ups under her real name, Hannah Ellis.

In a bid to get attention from her young sons, she decided to give children's books a try! Writing about dragons and talking animals was a big change from writing romantic comedies, but she enjoyed it very much.

Sparks was Hannah's Mum's childhood nickname and seemed like a fitting name for her children's books.

ABOUT THE ILLUSTRATOR

Katherine Newton works in various creative disciplines. Her themes and projects range from architecture, design, illustration, installation, video and music. The design and processes overlap in many projects.

If you would like to see more of Katherine's work please visit her website:

www.kpunktnewton.com

ALSO BY HANNAH SPARKS